KING OF THE JINNS

TAHIR SHAH

ANCA CHELARU

KING OF THE JINNS

TAHIR SHAH

ANCA CHELARU

MMXXIII

Secretum Mundi Publishing Ltd
124 City Road
London
EC1V 2NX
United Kingdom

www.secretum-mundi.com
info@secretum-mundi.com

First published by Secretum Mundi Publishing Ltd in
Daydreams of an Octopus & Other Stories, 2022
Published in this edition, 2023

KING OF THE JINNS

Artwork drawn by Anca Chelaru

A CIP catalogue record for this title is available from the BritishLibrary.

VERSION: 22112022

Visit the author's website:
Tahirshah.com

ISBN 978-1-914960-89-5

One

The Fruit Tree

LOOK AT MY hands if you need proof of a life misspent on the ocean swell.

Each one a mirror of the other, both are calloused and bleak, like the end of the world. They've been burned by ropes, chapped, battered, blistered, robbed of their nails and half their thumbs.

Those of us who call the ocean their world and a cluster of wretched bleached planks their land wouldn't trade the tumult of saline voyage for all the gems of the Orient. A taut sail thrusting us to the horizon is all we demand to bask in the glory of adventure.

And so it was that we set out from Sur, the veritable port of Sindbad.

Our ship was a ripened dhow, as fine and tested as any, our quest to trade a mountain of dates for the spices of the East.

The crew was a dozen souls, each one as weatherworn as the last, ruled over by a tyrant of a master. Never have I encountered such a malevolent captain, who took great pride in subjecting those under his command to misery and pain.

We sailed for forty horizons, the brightest daylight alternating with nightscapes as secret as any I've known. In all that time, we hardly passed another vessel or caught sight of even a single blade of grass. With each day that passed, the captain dreamed up new ways to visit discomfort on the fellow souls aboard.

He cut our rations, even though the stores of grain were plentiful.

When one of the barrels had sprung a leak, its precious contents draining away across the deck, he chose a man at random and whipped him until the poor wretch could no longer stand.

Then, one morning, the master gave the order to steer towards an archipelago, marked on the map as a dozen crumbs of grey amid an expanse of unyielding blue.

'We will set ashore for as long as it takes to find water and fruit,' he said. 'And any man who finds nothing will be left ashore.'

One of the deckhands spoke the word 'danger', at which the captain rolled his eyes.

'Uninhabited,' he said, the word spoken as a triumph of certainty.

'You sure?' questioned the cook.

The question saw him whipped for gross insubordination.

As we circumnavigated the first of the islands we encountered, we took in the luxurious vegetation and rocky outcrops from a distance. It seemed that the captain was right – not a single sign of humanity.

Drawing closer, we skulked up to a beach on the leeward side, and one at a time we waded ashore, each one of us unarmed, the golden-yellow sand tantalizing to our feet.

I can hardly describe the delight at exchanging the slip-sliding deck for that dry, unyielding beach.

We must have stood there for an hour, marvelling at it, as though we were taking in a magnificent mural fashioned from the furthest limits of imagination.

'Paradise,' the captain announced, flopping down in the shade of the palms.

'You can leave me here to live out my days,' said another.

'That's what I've got a mind to do!' uttered the master.

‘I’ll go in search for water,’ the cook grunted, his back still dripping in blood.

‘And I will look for fruit,’ I said. ‘I’d give my right arm for a juicy peach.’

The rest of the crew got to work with all the chores dry land makes possible. They were truly content – singing, laughing, and strolling about with the gait of delirious delight.

Tramping off into the undergrowth, I took in the rare and bewitching cornucopia of vegetation.

My mind’s eye imagined a tree covered in a hundred fruits, each of them different from the next. There were cherries and peaches, grapefruits and apples, oranges, apricots, mangoes and fabulous green melons.

Forcing the pleasing apparition from my head, I kept going, weaving a path between the palms and the boulders. I'm not sure why, but I was drawn to the left, into a copse of hardwood trees, their boughs festooned in shafts of sunlight.

My ears picked up the sound of an insect buzzing nearby. You will think me mad, but I swear it was calling out in warning:

'Turn back! Turn back! Or you shall pay the price for curiosity!'

Swatting the creature away from my face, I squinted to focus on the distance.

The mixture of dazzling light and darkness was playing tricks on me.

I rubbed a hand down over my eyes and looked again.

A few feet away was a marvellous tree – laden with every imaginable fruit. Breathing in sharply, I assumed it was a mirage conjured from my imagination.

But, on reaching it, I found the tree to be real.

The mangoes and the melons, the apples, oranges, peaches, and plums – more delicious than anything my tongue had ever tasted. The tree's magic was more remarkable still. For, whenever I plucked one of the fruits, it grew back immediately – replaced by an exact copy of itself.

As I stood there, a peach in one hand, a mango in the other, and a plum in my mouth, the insect sounded the alarm once again.

'Turn back! Turn back! Turn back now while you still can!'

A second time, I swished the annoying creature away. And when it was gone, I harvested a fine quantity of the fruit, delighting in the way it regrew as if by magic.

Once I had an ample haul, I set about crafting a basket from palm fronds.

Within a few minutes, I was ready to return to the beach in triumph.

As I raised my foot to take the first stride, the insect buzzed around my face a third time – far more urgently than before.

Infuriated at anything lying between me and the shore, I swatted it.

Suddenly, everything I'd ever known was flipped inside out and back to front.

The sky was replaced by the undergrowth, and the undergrowth by the sky.

The trunks of trees were leaves, and the leaves were trunks.

The shade was light, and the light was shade.

But, most alarming of all, the fruits in my homemade basket were no longer fruits – but rather the severed, bloodied heads of miniature people.

In horror, I hurled the basket down, the grotesque contents tumbling out across the sky. As they collided with the clouds, they screamed, as though I had slaughtered them.

Gripped by terror, I fled.

At breakneck speed, I retraced the zigzagging path between the palms and the boulders, all of them rooted in the sky. Far behind, the muffled screams of the dismembered grew all the louder.

Like an athlete moving in a desperate attempt to shatter a record, I ran faster than I'd ever run before.

In the distance I made out the beach, and the ocean beyond it – each hanging upside down.

I was about to cry out to the master, who was stretched out beneath palms, the sky beneath him.

But, as my lungs filled with air with which to make my exclamation, the sky flipped back in place, the ground opened up, and I descended into an abyss.

Two

The Lair

I FELL…

…and I fell.

And I fell some more… my lungs swollen, screaming like a babe in arms.

As I screamed, and screamed, and fell, I thought of every imaginable thing I had ever seen.

I thought of fat-tailed sheep roasting on spits.

Of a hanged man, bloated and black.

A wrecked ship, the crew picked clean by sharks.

Sixteen letters written in the ink of true love.

A hermit's cave halfway up a precipice.

Ocean waves the size of mountains.

The face of a child as innocent as a summer dawn.

And I thought of ten thousand other things, each of them as insignificant as the last.

Then, against the cacophonous roar of hooves charging over stone…

Blackness.

A terrible and infernal blackness.

Not merely an absence of light, but a dark that was somehow tethered to the most exasperating strains of wickedness.

And with the blackness came a collision.

A collision between my flailing, floundering self, and a kind of rock.

Or, rather, as I was to discover, a tunnel wall.

Striking it full pelt, I was almost knocked unconscious, reeling in pain and consternation.

'Silence!' cried a voice as cold and dark as the bewildering realm in which I found myself.

'Where am I?' I groaned.

The moist leather tongue of a whip struck me in the ribs.

Crouching there, terrified, I could only hope in ardent desperation to wake from a dream.

The whip lashed again, cracking like thunder.

I whimpered, muffling a palm to my mouth. As I did so, I felt a hand grasping hold of me and pulling me sideways. Shaking, cringing, weeping, I pleaded to be spared.

'Don't make a sound!' hissed a voice in a forced whisper. 'Not until the guard's gone.'

'What guard?'

'*Shush!*'

The hand that had grabbed hold of me forced me down low, so as to protect me.

Still reeling, I was drenched through from fear.

I squatted there for what seemed like an eternity, my ears filled with the sound of hammers rasping on stone, my nostrils plugged with the vile scent of sulphur.

As the minutes slipped into hours, my eyes adjusted to the blackness.

I have no idea how I was able to see anything, but I could, not that it provided relief.

I was in a tunnel no taller than the height of a man, the walls adorned with a gallery of misfortune and death.

Leering, jeering faces clung to crushed skulls.

All of a sudden, the blackness lifted.

'The guard's gone,' said the voice.

'I can see now,' I answered.

'Of course you can, because the guard's cloak has moved away.'

'Where is this, and who are you?'

'You're in the Lair, and I am Rastec.'

The answers led to a dozen more questions.

Piece by piece I learned a few basic fragments of information…

The Lair was a labyrinthine prison-mine owned by Stalid-Jak, King of the Jinns.

Those unfortunate enough to have been trapped there, by plucking fruits from one of his many trees, had no hope of ever escaping. Prisoners served out their lives by crushing rocks so that Stalid-Jak could amass a fortune in a mineral without a purpose or a name.

Rastec had been a sailor like me, before being trapped on an island far from the one on which I'd harvested fruit.

A short man, his hair grey with age, his voice as rough as granite, he had an apologetic demeanour, as though repentant for everything he uttered.

'How long have you been here?' I asked.

'Since my youth.'

'And how have you survived?'

Rastec looked at me hard, his eyes filled with terror. Not a passing fear, but terror.

'I've endured this limbo for decades by making every day an adventure in itself,' he said.

'That doesn't make sense.'

'It may not now,' he responded. 'But languish in the Lair for as long as I have, and you'll come to understand it to be the key.'

'The key to what?'

'The key to survival,' Rastec said.

Three

The Labyrinth

Day after day, I toiled for Stalid-Jak, even though there were no days or nights in that abhorrent netherworld.

I lived in the moment, and learned from Rastec's example, regarding each new day as a glorious new adventure.

While the other prisoners were pushed down lower and lower, I learned to rise up, and to see wonder in almost everything.

When hammering at the rock face, I delighted in the way the stone would splinter off in shards. I drew pleasure, too, in observing the droplets of water shimmering and gleaming on the tunnel walls. But most of all, I took comfort in the mysterious by-lines that formed the labyrinth.

At first, I imagined that the prison-mine was no more than a few hundred yards of tunnel. After all, to the untrained eye, one stretch looked very much the same as another.

As weeks turned to months, I began to comprehend the vast and interlocking scale. Rastec taught me to mark the labyrinth as I went, so as to remind myself of stretches I'd explored before.

The other prisoners, except for Rastec and me, would collapse as soon as their daily toil at the rock face was over. Each of them was a spent force, a dead man waiting to have the last breath squeezed from his chest.

Hammering at the rock, as I was obliged to do hour after hour, I would be charged with anticipation. The thought of exploring once my hammer had been passed to the next shift was a life force in itself.

As time passed, I discovered vast new swathes of the labyrinth, mapping them so that I could return again and again.

A great many of the tunnels were former mine shafts, while others appeared to be natural. I found pools of crystal-clear water, petrified forests, and burial grounds. Eventually, as my confidence strengthened all the more, I located the zone reserved for the jinns.

Confiding in Rastec, I revealed how I planned to escape from the mine and see how far I could get – crossing into the realm where the jinns roamed.

'No human has ever reached the jinn zone and survived to tell the tale,' he replied ominously.

'Why not?'

'Because the King of the Jinns will smell you. And, when he's smelled you, he'll catch you and boil down your bones.'

I sighed in ecstasy.

‘A single moment of freedom would surely be superior to a lifetime of slavery, would it not?’ I answered.

‘Perhaps. But if you vanish, they’ll hunt you. I’ve seen it happen. You’ll be dragged to Stalid-Jak, and then he’ll…’

‘I know! He’ll boil up my bones!’

Rastec’s eyes glistened in fear.

‘That’s only when he’s finished making an example of you.’

And so, for a hundred more days, I toiled at the rock face, exploring the labyrinth farther and farther, pushing the boundaries of my knowledge.

One night, while wandering through the maze, I reached the limit of my map.

Without realizing it, I strayed into the jinn zone.

Thinking about it now, I should have known from the moment I stepped across the threshold that I was free from the mines. The reason wasn't the smell, or the fact there were no prisoners there – but rather that the half-light had lifted. And, as I progressed, the gloom was replaced by sunshine.

Bathed in dazzling light, I made my way through a canyon, towering walls sheering up on either side like the ramparts of a great citadel. I was about to turn on my heel and hurry back to the slave quarters when something caught my eye.

A nest.

Not an ordinary one, but rather, a nest so vast in scale that it took me a good long while to comprehend it was a nest at all. The size of a house, it was lodged in a cleft halfway up one of the precipitous canyon walls. Rising up, its girth splayed outwards, throwing an ominous shadow over the rock on which it perched.

I noticed something delicate and black flapping from one side.

Craning my neck, I tried to get a better view.

Impelled by curiosity and unable to resist, I strolled over to the sheering rock wall and began to climb.

The life of a seafarer is the one of a mountaineer.

Aboard ship, I was forever scaling the mast, smoothing the sail, untangling the ropes. Within a handful of minutes, I'd covered the distance between the canyon's floor and the nest.

My eyes dazzled by shafts of sunlight, I discerned that the black material was actually a garment – a cloak. Approaching from the side, I observed how it was embroidered with pure gold thread. A moment after that I realized that the cloak was the vestment of an unfortunate victim, whose bones littered the nest.

Perched there, I regained my breath and looked out at a panorama as magnificent as any I'd ever spied on land. There were mountains crested with daubs of crisp white snow, forests and jungles, deserts – and beyond them all, an ocean.

As I feasted on that sight of water, iridescent and otherworldly, my ears reported an alarmed warning – the distant sound of a bird high in the heavens above.

All of a sudden, the sun was masked, and a shadow descended over me – a shadow tinged in the coldest, darkest fear.

Thrusting my head back, I set eyes on a colossal winged harbinger of death.

The creature's talons were sharp as razors, its beak hooked and cruel like an armament from Roman warfare.

Ripping a forked branch from the side of the nest, I swung it left and right.

The more I did so, the more the raptor was spurred on to avenge my intrusion.

In ten thousand adventures I cannot remember fighting so fiercely to save my throat from being torn out.

The giant bird – a roc – ascended, rising up high into the firmament.

Then she plunged…

Down, down, down…

Both wings tucked in tight.

That moment is etched on my memory like nothing else.

Reviewing it, as I do each night, I salute it as a sight of utter wonder. Had I stood there frozen to the spot, gaping a moment longer, I would not be sitting here, retelling the tale.

As the last seconds of my life elasticated, I threw myself into action, struggling to come up with a plan. Any plan, however faulty it may have been, was better than resigning myself to instant death.

I don't know how or why I thought of it, but something deep within me seemed to offer a solution.

A nonsensical, wretched solution.

'Put on the cloak,' it whispered, 'and empty your mind.'

The roc was so close now that I could see the speckled breast feathers and blood-covered talons.

With a single movement made at breakneck speed, I tugged the cloak from the nest, wrapped it around me, crouched lower than low, and cleared my mind.

Silence.

Cold, bone-numbing silence.

Four

Jinn Zone

Cowering there in darkness, I waited for the moment of impact...

...the moment in which I was to be ripped limb from limb.

But the creature didn't strike.

Was it holding back in an ultimate, elevated form of torture?

A full excruciating minute of worry and wonder slipped by, each second a year in itself. As it did so, I fought to keep the stage of my mind clear, as instructed by the whisper.

Unable to resist any longer, I lined a blinking eye up with a hole in the cloak and peeked out.

No sign of the roc, or its nest, or even of the canyon far below.

No sign of anything that had been there a moment before.

In a mystifying act of sorcery, the cloak had delivered me in the nick of time from the clutches of death.

Shaking, I clambered uneasily to my feet, jerking the mantle from my shoulders.

'What horror of horrors is this, my new tormentor?' I voiced aloud.

Setting eyes upon my new circumstances, I grasped with immediate and distressed attention that I was a prisoner yet again.

Although the raptor and its abode were apparently far away, the place in which I found myself was equally as terrible as the raptor's nest, or indeed, the wretched netherworld of the mines.

As far as I could make out, I was at the bottom of a well – an empty well. Spiralling up to greet the faintest pinprick of light, its walls were as indomitable as those of a great fortress.

My eyes adjusting to the dimness once again, I discerned that I was not standing on firm ground, but rather upon the dismembered remains of the dead.

Never before have I begged Providence to rob me of my sight as I did in that sordid purgatory. I'd have plucked out my eyes right there and then had the whisper not come a second time.

'Search…' it said.

I growled, then groaned, and growled again.

'Search for *what*?!'

'Search for the key.'

I began to weep, tears rolling down my cheeks. And as I wept, I giggled. Not the merriment of joy, but that of a madman, pushed to the furthest, most haunting limits of sanity.

The cloak may have saved me from being ripped apart, but it had only done so in order to preserve me long enough to perish in an even more gruesome way.

'There are no keys here!' I cried. 'You siren of damnation! I curse you for not allowing me to be ridded of life in the canyon, as Fate had surely wished me to be!'

'Search for the key,' the whisper spoke a third time.

Seething with rage, I swung my arms around, as if whooshing away a swarm of hornets.

I would have uttered another imprecation, but a clamour came from above, startling me.

Looking up, I saw a commotion high above, played out in the telescoped dot of light. A moment after that, objects were plummeting down into the well, impelled by the rawest manifestation of gravity.

Bouncing to and fro against the brick walls, they came to a sudden stop, their contents spilling out all around to where I was standing. No great investigation in the half-light was necessary to identify them as carcasses that had once borne human names.

Slipping about in the putrid remains, I cursed the whisper when, again, it spoke the familiar line:

'Search for the key.'

My mind was wiped clean of anguish, like a child's writing slate washed at a river's edge.

Collapsing to my knees, I witnessed myself from a great height, as though perhaps viewed from the far end of the well. But rather than being the size of an ant, the perception was as viewed through an eyeglass.

There I was, covered top to toe in battered human offal, sinew, and blood, the only live creature for a thousand feet of damnation.

Watching myself with deft curiosity, I was intrigued at my pathetic state. I had begged divine Providence to rid me of my sight.

And, while it seemed not to have done so, I *was* blind – at least to the possibility of blessed salvation.

Five

Key, Lock

STARING DOWN, MY eyes were open wider than at any time I'd known.

Not only could I see myself there, but I could hear myself, smell myself, and even experience the touch of my own kith and kin.

But that was only the beginning.

You see, through some inexplicable force of illusion, I could peer into the frail life force of my own soul. Sensing my fears and ambitions, I read my personal histories, my darkest secrets, and my dreams.

In other circumstances, the investigations would have gripped my attention. Yet, as I floundered there in that shaft of demise, I noticed something which had escaped my attention until then.

Mounted on the wall, beside where I was standing, was a wooden door.

In the middle of it was a keyhole.

A neat, circular keyhole in urgent need of a circular key.

Throwing my hands up in the air, I cursed the whispered voice, the stench of death, and my own doomed existence. How on earth was I supposed to find a key in a mound of dismembered bodies?

I collapsed onto the bones once again and screamed until I was hoarse.

The despair would surely have blinded me, but it ceased in the blink of an eye.

Despair was exchanged instantly for a single yet dazzling ray of overwhelming hope.

Hope that came not as an idea or a stray thought, but in the form of a key hanging on a hook an inch or two to the left of the portal.

As soon as my gaze fixed upon it, the view from above vanished.

I was returned to my own self, my full and absolute concentration preoccupied with the key. Thinking about it as I'm doing now, I glided up to where it was suspended.

Rather than snatching it in some ungrateful show of force, I approached in awe, and with unspoken blessings.

The key was to be revered, to be honoured, to be loved.

Stammering out thanks, both spoken and mute, I pressed my face right up to it.

The light was dim, and my mood was one of soothed desperation, but the key was not what I would have expected in a million turbulent dreams.

Circular, it appeared to bear the exact circumference needed to fit the lock.

But it was not a key as I had ever known a key to be.

A dismembered human finger, its prolonged, sharpened nail was etched in an elaborate geometric design.

Without giving it a second thought, I lifted the finger, the flesh strangely warm to the touch. My own fingers trembling, I bore it up to the door with reverence and slipped it into the keyhole.

You will think me deranged in saying it, but I swear the key understood what was taking place, that it propelled itself into the lock and rotated a full turn to the right.

Whether it did, or whether in my deranged state I simply imagined it, hardly mattered.

All that mattered was that the key opened the lock.

Summoning all my strength, I prepared to force the portal wide open.

But there was no need.

As soon as the key had turned, the door swung open.

Framed in the aperture in which it sat was a scene I knew better than my own face… a scene I love as a son loves his mother, like the comforting embrace of a long-lost friend.

A vast and iridescent sea.

Six

Hope

As I MADE my way down to the shore, I strived to make sense of the roc's nest, the cloak, the well, and the lock that had opened when the finger had slipped inside.

No amount of pondering brought me any closer to a conclusion. All I could do was to honour the unknown forces of the universe, and to prostrate myself before them.

For all my high opinions, I was nothing more than the tiniest and most insignificant speck of grit on the face of a distant star.

So, wandering down to the water, I crossed a blackened crest of rocks, dipped a hand in the liquid, and touched a few drops to my mouth.

To my astonishment, it was not brine, but fresh water.

Think of it… a lake that appeared as expansive as a sea, the surface shimmering as though viewed through a kaleidoscope.

Salivating at the prospect of not merely inspecting it from a distance, but being cupped upon it on a vessel, I set about wondering how to make a boat of some kind.

Before I knew it, my imagination had designed the perfect dhow – its sleek lines fashioned from exquisite timber, its sails taut in the breeze.

No sooner had the thought entered my head, than a dhow floated gently into view.

The very same dhow I had imagined.

It wasn't the usual kind of derelict craft I'd known in two decades hunkered before the sail. Rather, it was magnificent as magnificent can be. Its timber was caulked, its sails made from the finest blinding-white cloth.

I stood there, grinning to myself like a madman cackling at the wind.

As my eyes feasted on every inch of wood, something caught my attention, warming my heart.

Inscribed on the bow was my name – *Abdur Rahman.*

On reading the appellation, all apprehension I may have had at climbing aboard melted. Wading into the water, I grabbed hold of a trailing rope and ascended.

From the first moment my feet pressed down on the deck, it was as though air was breathed back into my lungs, raising me from the dead.

A sailor without a sea beneath them is like a farmer in the city, or a man from the mountains lost on an interminable plain.

Exploring the ship, *my* ship, I found her stocked with all manner of provisions and supplies: fresh melons, coconuts, dates, fifty drums of water, and enough sacks of rice to feed an army.

Never in all my dreams and unbridled fantasies had I imagined such a thing.

Sucking the elation deep into my lungs, I reproached myself for mislaying hope before. How foolish I'd been not to remember that, even when all is lost, a stray wisp of hope always remains for those brave enough to believe.

No sooner than I was ready, the dhow set off towards the horizon. There was no need to steer her, to trim the sails, for she seemed to respond to my thoughts.

Within an hour, *Abdur Rahman* and I were under sail, slicing through the water, the sun glinting overhead, my spirits rejuvenated like never before.

For three days and nights we pushed on.

I had no idea where I was, or where that vessel bearing my name was destined. The thing that intrigued me was that it appeared certain to know where it was headed.

From time to time, the ropes adjusted themselves, and the sails were trimmed or reconfigured to pick up a fresh breeze sweeping in from the west.

On some occasions, I gave an unspoken command, only to hear a whisper of apology ringing in my ears while the rudder was forced in the opposite direction.

At dawn on the fourth morning, *Abdur Rahman* reduced its speed.

We were far from the nearest island or shore of any kind. I gave the order to keep moving at full speed, but however many times I insisted we push on, the dhow slowed.

Irritated at having my orders challenged, I stamped my foot on the deck.

'Trust in me,' the whisper said.

'There's a good wind, so let's make use of it!' I snapped.

'But we have arrived, Master,' the voice responded.

'*Arrived*? Arrived where?'

'At the place where you are destined to be.'

Seven

King of the Jinns

As soon as the words had been whispered, the anchor lowered, and the temperature of the air rose sharply.

Within less time than it takes to tell, the climate shifted from that of a crisp spring day to oppressive tropical heat. Opening one of the caskets, I ladled cool water over my head.

Standing there on the deck, I waited like a fool for something to happen. I was about to launch into a castigation of the dhow when the deck began to tremble.

At first it was almost too slight to be discernible. But, as moments became minutes, it grew more pronounced. Soon it was less of a trembling and more of a rocking – a rocking that shifted into a frenzy of side-to-side jolting.

I grasped hold of the rail as my namesake was thrust left, right, left.

And as the craft juddered and shuddered about, the expanse of water beyond the keel crested in waves as high as any I've spied in a life wedded to the sea.

As I watched, a sharp little rock protruded through the water not fifty yards from where the *Abdur Rahman* was anchored.

I assumed the swell had retreated, revealing its jagged outline.

But I was wrong.

Oh, how I was wrong.

For as the jerking and the jolting continued, and waves splashed and sighed, the rock kept on rising.

My eyes fixed upon it.

Like the intended prey of some great carnivore on the savannah, I couldn't help but be obsessed about it – wondering how and why it could be pushing up from the deep.

All the while, the jagged rock ascended.

Soon it wasn't merely a rock, but more of a boulder.

Within minutes, it was less of a boulder and more of a monolith – freestanding on an island of its own.

And it kept rising, the waves around it draining away as land replaced them.

As I watched that miracle of miracles, my beloved vessel became marooned – not on the shore, but halfway up the mountain that had reared up through the waves.

A mountain which in actual fact was not a mountain at all, but rather a monumental throne.

As I stood there, my lower jaw hanging in stupefaction, my mind was too fatigued to race or wonder any more. I fell to my knees on the slanted deck, as I had done on the crushed bodies in the well.

It was all I could muster: a last exhausted pledge of submission to a higher authority.

The moment my skin pressed down on the wood, that power, that being, that pillar of omnipotence, revealed itself.

In my adventures, I've encountered giants and ifrits, ogres, ghouls, and all manner of jinns. Many of them were cruel, or ugly, or cruel *and* ugly, but none could match the monstrous beast perched before me on that imperious cathedra.

The grotesque head was governed by a single eye – gaping, grey, and framed in scales. Shadowed by an overpowering brow, it seemed to drink in the landscape, as if sensible to the fact it was the laird of all it surveyed.

Below the eye were three fluted nostrils, the horn of some primeval rhinoceros arming each one. On either side of the face was mounted a miniature ear, no more than an afterthought. Like every other inch of flesh, they were scaled – prepared for battle.

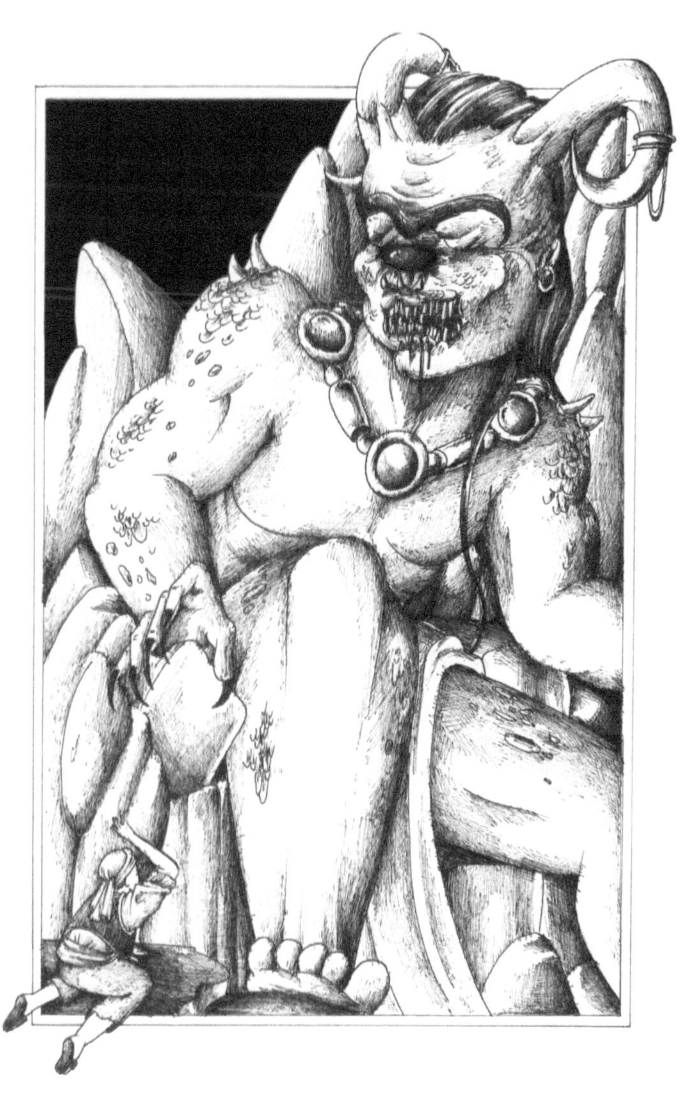

But it was the beast's mouth that commanded my attention most. In all the years that have elapsed since I set eyes upon it, I have wondered how I would ever begin to provide a description of that infernal orifice.

Encircling the opening like a bulwark, the lips were cracked, their flesh fetid and haggard as though cursed by the forces of hell. Beyond them was a realm of destruction – rows and rows of teeth, the likes of which I have never seen or imagined in a thousand nightmares. Each one was a different size and shape, bonded to all the others in a grand fraternity of horror; rinsed in vile, unearthly saliva resembling blood.

'Did you really believe I would spare you?' the mouth spoke.

'Who… who… who are you?' I faltered, amazed at myself for daring to address it at all.

'I am your master... the one you sought to escape.'

'Escape? From where?' I spluttered.

'From the mines.'

My heart missed a beat, then another.

'*You're...*' I couldn't spit the words out. Swallowing, I tried a second time, then a third... 'You're Stalid-Jak.... *King... King... King of the Jinns!*'

The beast did not reply, not in words. Instead, he leaned back into the throne that was the mountain, his singular eye brooding.

'Are you going to boil up my bones?' I asked – not because I was especially interested to know, but rather as a way of clutching to life for the moment an answer would provide.

The King of the Jinns scanned the far horizon.

In his own time, his line of sight roamed closer...

Over the expanse of sea glinting with sunlight, across the narrow ribbon of shore, up across the foothills of the mountain, over the decks of the marooned dhow, and onto my face.

For a full minute he looked upon me.

In the space of that insignificant interval, I was thrown into turmoil.

A turmoil consuming me, I felt as though I were being eaten from the inside, ripped apart and devoured.

I have no comprehension of what actually occurred, but it felt as though my heart had swelled to twice its normal size; that my veins and arteries were stretched out mile upon mile; that every nerve, sinew, bone, and ligament was compacted upon the next.

All this merely from being observed by that gargantuan and unearthly eye.

‘I’m no more than a humble sailor from a distant land,’ I crooned, my voice pitiful and weak. ‘If you are to dispatch me, O King of the Jinns, please have mercy and make my end swift in the name of compassion.’

The beast’s immense form seemed to writhe in pleasure at the utterance.

Ruminating with hideous delight, he thrust both paws out and then up – splaying the scaled, elongated digits as though they were swords.

‘Were I to allow a prisoner to escape the retribution awaiting him,’ the King of the Jinns answered, ‘I would be a laughing stock! And besides, there are few pleasures in life quite as satisfying as exacting revenge on a poor, snivelling wretch such as you.’

‘Oh, Great Master,’ I yelled at the top of my voice so as to be heard at all. ‘How can a humble seafarer such as me provide satisfaction for one as mighty as you? After all, I’m less than nothing in the grand scheme of creation!’

The King of the Jinns peered out to the horizon, his gaze slowly retracting over the waves, the shore, and the rocks, and back onto my face.

‘I shall snuff out your life in any way I see fit!’ he roared, the words howling at me like a winter squall.

‘Then take me,’ I said, bearing my neck so that it might be severed.

The beast seemed to grin.

‘For all your bravado at daring to escape my labyrinth, you are as pitiful as any other man!’

‘Oh no, Great One,’ I spoke, ‘I am weaker, and frailer, and more deserving of execution than any other creature you have pitted yourself against.’

‘At last you speak Truth,’ said the King of the Jinns.

Bowing my head, my eyes trained low on the wooden deck, I made peace with my Creator, and prepared to make the journey to His realm.

Eight

The Mechanism

As I KNELT there, the beast no doubt deciding how best to make an example of a fugitive prisoner, a stray thought slipped onto the stage of my exhausted consciousness.

When I had imagined the dhow, *my* dhow – the one which bore my name – it had appeared… just like that, a radiant and exact facsimile of the vessel I had glimpsed in my mind's eye.

Either I had dreamt it, along with everything else in that absurd version of reality… or there was, by some inexplicable alchemy, a mysterious force at work.

A force that enabled the imagination to conjure events.

My brow furrowing as I considered these questions, my neck still bared in the direction of the Great Jinn's gaze, I struggled to stand.

At seeing me on my feet, the King of the Jinns called out:

'I hear that execution is all the swifter in the kneeling position.'

I didn't reply, for I was too preoccupied with imagining a machine.

Within the blink of an eye it was standing before me, the sides of its convoluted mechanism catching the light. The size of a wagon drawn by six horses, it was covered in metal pipes and tubes, a marvel of complexity.

I showed no surprise in its arrival. Nor did I feel the need to examine it – after all, it had been summoned into existence from plans I had myself created.

But as soon as the object appeared on the dhow's slanted deck, the beast grunted.

He didn't deign to enquire what it was doing there, or indeed what it was… but I could sense his curiosity feasting upon it.

'Well…?' he said at length. 'What is it?'

'Oh,' I shrugged with nonchalance, 'nothing at all, really. Just a device… an amusement… a fanciful creation.'

'What is its purpose?' the King of the Jinns asked, his curiosity piqued.

'As I say, it's an amusement and nothing more,' I replied.

'But it must have a function,' the beast insisted.

'It does, of course, but in these strained circumstances, and things being what they are, there's hardly a point in going into the details, is there?'

'Explain its purpose,' the Great One said, 'and…'

‘*And…?*’

‘And I shall give you a few minutes’ delay before I end your life.’

Recoiling back on the slanted deck, I rolled my eyes.

‘There’s really no point,’ I said. ‘You see, you’re going to kill me – so nothing else really matters. I’d actually be grateful if you would get on with the execution. You may think me unhinged, but I have been looking forward to meeting my Creator. You could chalk it down to my own curiosity.’

That final word hung in the air.

I could feel the King of the Jinns breathing it in, holding it in his infernal lungs.

‘All right,’ he said, his voice fuelled by rage, ‘show me what it does and I shall consider setting you free.’

I burst out in pained laughter.

'Thank you, but considering setting me free is not the same as actually setting me free – so I will pass on the offer.'

Again, the beast grunted.

As he did so, the heavens above the brine darkened with storm clouds.

The grunt extended into a growl, and the growl into a roar of indignation – a roar that was itself mirrored in the sky.

'I could sever your throat and then work out what the machine is for,' said the beast.

'Perhaps that's so,' I responded, 'but it's complex. See all the pipes and the tubes for yourself.'

'It may seem complicated to the limited faculties of a sailor, but to the dazzling genius of a jinn, it's nothing at all.'

'As I've already told you, I'm quite prepared to be slain as the penalty for escaping. So, let's get on with it, shall we?'

The King of the Jinns raised himself off the throne.

Continuing my charade, I pretended to be unimpressed by his colossal height, or by the fact his grotesque scaled form was slippery with blood.

'Show me how the mechanism is operated, and I shall give you your freedom,' he said, each word framed in the purest rage.

'Very well,' I said, 'but please remember you may not be amused by what you find.'

'I shall decide whether I am amused or not!' Stalid-Jak boomed.

Raising a hand above my head, I yelled:

'How can I be certain you will not swindle me?'

The beast clapped his paws together, thunder ringing out over the sea.

'What do you know about the souls of jinns?' he asked.

Stepping back, I brushed the tip of a finger to my chin.

'That they take the form of a bird,' I said, 'and that a jinn cannot be captured unless its soul is caged.'

Stalid-Jak made a fist of his paw and shook it in my direction.

A moment later, a little sparrow was perched on the deck within arm's reach.

I looked at the bird, then up at the King of the Jinns.

'*Is that…?*'

The jinn blinked, as if to confirm that the sparrow was his soul.

'If I trick you,' he said, 'you would be able to take vengeance on that frail little bird.'

Drawing a hand down over my face, I sighed.

'What a pity,' I said.

The great beast clenched both paws into fists and scowled.

'Hurry up and reveal the intricacies of the mechanism, or I'll grind you into dust!'

'I would at once,' I said, another sigh escaping from my lips. 'But, alas, I need a little creature for the demonstration.'

'What kind of creature?'

'Well, something small and intelligent… something like a mouse, a lizard, or a small bird.'

At that moment, as if cued to do so, the sparrow let out a tweet.

'Now I think of it, your soul would be perfect for the demonstration,' I said. 'It won't be harmed. I give you my word.'

Stalid-Jak seethed with irritation and impatience.

'Very well, but only if you promise.'

I did so, opening a flap in the side of the machine.

'Please ask your soul to step inside,' I said.

Even before the words had left my mouth, the sparrow had flown over to the contraption and scurried inside.

With care, I closed the flap, slid a bolt into place, and secured it with a padlock.

'Welcome to your new home,' I said, breaking into a smile.

The mountain-throne casting a shadow behind him, Stalid-Jak, King of the Jinns, thrust both fists above his head, summoning all his strength.

All I could wonder was whether he planned to grind me into dust, boil up my bones, or dispatch me in any other way.

Whatever his dastardly intention, it was no matter.

For, his soul having been trapped, the great beast was as powerless to extinguish my life as he was to free the little sparrow from the machine.

The bird tweeted for a moment or two, then something happened which took me by surprise.

The King of the Jinns melted into the rocks, like a candle left out in the sun.

As he did so, time was reversed at high speed.

The throne, and the mountain that formed it, submerged into the earth and disappeared. With the island gone, the sea roamed back to where it had before.

My dhow zigzagged in reverse across a kaleidoscope of horizons.

I slipped back through the portal into the well.

Then, furling around me, the cloak transported me to the roc's nest.

I descended to the base of the canyon.

Having reversed my way through the jinn zone, I reached the labyrinth, Rastec, and the infernal mine.

A moment after that, as though it were quite normal to relive past experiences in reverse, I was hurtling up through the abyss.

Once again, the sky was the ground, and the ground was the sky.

And before I knew it, I was back at the fruit tree, the spot at which it had all begun.

Standing there, I dipped my head in wonder and in awe.

The journey had been dreadful. But, as I reflected, there is nothing in this life that does not provide a lesson of consummate value.

Retracing my steps through the undergrowth, I reached the shore.

The ship's master was still lying beneath the palms, and the other crew members busy with their chores.

'Where's all the fruit you promised us?' the captain barked, with one eye open and the other closed. 'I'll whip you if you don't tell me you have found fruit aplenty.'

Looking at that cruel, tempestuous excuse of a man through narrowed eyes, I forced a smile.

‘I found the most wonderful fruit tree, sir. Never seen anything like it. But the remarkable thing is that it asked for you by name.’

The master sat up.

‘Take me to it,’ he said angrily.

‘At once, Master,’ I replied.

Finis

About the Author

Descended from a long line of storytellers, writers, and savants, Tahir Shah is one of the most prolific authors of his generation. He has published more than sixty books in numerous genres, including travel, fiction, and fantasy, as well as tales for children.

Raised in the tradition of Eastern 'teaching stories', Shah is passionate about stories and storytelling. He regards the ability to learn from folklore as being in us all, what he calls a 'default setting of humankind'. As well as having written scores of books, Shah has made documentaries for National Geographic TV and The History Channel. He is the founder and CEO of the charity, The Scheherazade Foundation.

About the Artist

Anca Chelaru grew up in a small town in Romania, where she picked up a passion for art and stories from her family's extensive library. She studied at the Ion Mincu University of Architecture and Urban Planning in Bucharest, and soon began pursuing her interest in book illustration – with a particular interest in fantasy and the surreal. Her main sources of artistic inspiration are the art nouveau movement and the post-war Romanian illustrators.

Books By Tahir Shah

Travel

Trail of Feathers
Travels With Myself
Beyond the Devil's Teeth
In Search of King Solomon's Mines
House of the Tiger King
In Arabian Nights
The Caliph's House
Sorcerer's Apprentice
Journey Through Namibia

Novels

Jinn Hunter: Book One – The Prism
Jinn Hunter: Book Two – The Jinnslayer
Jinn Hunter: Book Three – The Perplexity
Hannibal Fogg and the Supreme Secret of Man
Hannibal Fogg and the Codex Cartographica
Casablanca Blues
Eye Spy
Godman
Paris Syndrome
Timbuctoo

Nasrudin

Travels With Nasrudin
The Misadventures of the Mystifying Nasrudin
The Peregrinations of the Perplexing Nasrudin
The Voyages and Vicissitudes of Nasrudin
Nasrudin in the Land of Fools

Teaching Stories

The Arabian Nights Adventures

Scorpion Soup

Tales Told to a Melon

The Afghan Notebook

The Caravanserai Stories

Ghoul Brothers

Hourglass

Imaginist

Jinn's Treasure

Jinnlore

Mellified Man

Skeleton Island

Wellspring

When the Sun Forgot to Rise

Outrunning the Reaper

The Cap of Invisibility

On Backgammon Time

The Wondrous Seed

The Paradise Tree

Mouse House

The Hoopoe's Flight

The Old Wind

A Treasury of Tales

Daydreams of an Octopus & Other Stories

Miscellaneous

The Reason to Write

Zigzag Think

Being Myself

Research

Cultural Research

The Middle East Bedside Book

Three Essays

Anthologies

The Anthologies

The Clockmaker's Box

The Tahir Shah Fiction Reader

The Tahir Shah Travel Reader

Edited by

Congress With a Crocodile

A Son of a Son, Volume I

A Son of a Son, Volume II

Screenplays

Casablanca Blues: The Screenplay

Timbuctoo: The Screenplay

A REQUEST

If you enjoyed this book, please review it on your favourite online retailer or review website.

Reviews are an author's best friend.

To stay in touch with Tahir Shah, and to hear about his upcoming releases before anyone else, please sign up for his mailing list:

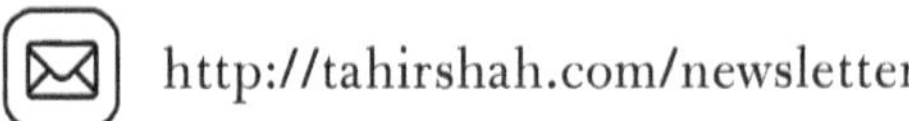

http://tahirshah.com/newsletter

And to follow him on social media, please go to any of the following links:

http://www.twitter.com/humanstew

@tahirshah999

http://www.facebook.com/TahirShahAuthor

http://www.youtube.com/user/tahirshah999

http://www.pinterest.com/tahirshah

https://www.goodreads.com/tahirshahauthor

http://www.tahirshah.com

www.ingramcontent.com/pod-product-compliance
Lightning Source LLC
Chambersburg PA
CBHW030522310726
48979CB00010B/1773/J

* 9 7 8 1 9 1 4 9 6 0 8 9 5 *